A Wint

Neil was leading Sam back into the kitchen from the freezing courtyard when a dreadful thought struck him. Where was Jake? He hurried on into the kitchen. It was empty. Though Neil looked under the table and in the spaces behind the fridge and the cooker, there was no sign of the vulnerable little pup.

Neil dashed out into the passage.

"Jake! Jake!" he called anxiously into the emptiness.

No little puppy scurried up to answer him. Everything was quiet.

Titles in the Puppy Patrol series

More Puppy Patrol stories follow soon

Puppy Patrol
A Winter's Tale

Jenny Dale

Illustrated by
Mick Reid

A Working Partners Book
MACMILLAN CHILDREN'S BOOKS

Special thanks to Cherith Baldry

First published 1998 by Macmillan Children's Books
a division of Macmillan Publishers Limited
25 Eccleston Place, London SW1W 9NF
and Basingstoke

Associated companies throughout the world

Created by Working Partners Limited
London W12 7QY

ISBN 0 330 37041 3

5 7 9 8 6 4

A CIP catalogue record for this book is available from
the British Library.

Typeset in Bookman Old Style by SX Composing DTP, Rayleigh, Essex
Printed and bound in Great Britain by Mackays of Chatham plc, Kent

Chapter One

"*D*ick *Whittington and his Dog?* What sort of pantomime is that?" Neil Parker pointed to a brightly coloured poster on the noticeboard and laughed. "What happened to the cat?"

"Who needs a cat?" his sister Emily said. "Denny's brilliant. He's our star pooch."

Neil and his mother, Carole Parker, along with Neil's five-year-old sister Sarah, had arrived at the church hall in Compton to collect Emily from her pantomime rehearsal. Every year the Compton Amateur Dramatic Society put on a special Christmas show for the local children, and this time Emily had a small part.

Neil had first met Denny, the golden retriever

1

in the pantomime, when a truck had hit the dog on the road just outside King Street Kennels. Gina Ward, who was in the year below Neil at Meadowbank School, had been walking Denny when the accident had happened. Neil had helped her to look after him while they waited for the vet. He didn't find out how clever Denny was until much later.

"Fudge is brilliant, too," said Sarah. "Why can't he be in the play?"

"*Dick Whittington and his Hamster?*" said Neil. "In your dreams, Squirt."

"Hamsters are too small," added Carole, as Sarah screwed up her face in a sulk. "No one in the audience would be able to see him."

Neil shifted his feet and looked around. The weather was icy cold outside, with snow expected, and the Church Hall felt distinctly chilly inside, even though he was wearing two sweaters, a padded jacket *and* a cap with ear-flaps pulled down over his spiky brown hair. He slapped his hands together in their woollen gloves.

Looking around, Neil could hardly believe that the pantomime would be ready in time for New Year's Eve, just ten days away – or that the cast had already been rehearsing for weeks.

The stage was bare except for a couple of chairs and a table, and the people standing in the middle of it were busy talking amongst themselves, not even trying to rehearse.

At the other end of the hall, Chris and Hasheem, two of Neil's friends from school, were sloshing paint onto a big canvas. In fact, Neil thought, Meadowbank School was well represented; his teacher, Paul Hamley, was there too, perched dangerously at the top of a ladder, fixing one of the stage lights.

"Are you going to be long?" Neil asked Emily. "I want to get back to King Street."

"I don't know."

Neil shifted again and looked impatiently at the hall clock. It was just coming up to half past five. "I've got to be home by six," he said. "Jane Hammond is bringing Jake."

Before Emily could reply, somebody called her, and she dashed off towards the stage. Neil turned back to where Carole was sitting on one of the hall chairs against the wall.

"Mum, I've got to be home by six," he repeated.

Carole was staring in front of her, not taking any notice of Neil. "I've posted the last of the Christmas cards . . ." She ticked the item off on her fingers. "I've collected the turkey. I've bought the veg, the chocolates and – gift wrap! I've forgotten the gift wrap!"

"Oh, Mum . . ."

Carole Parker gathered up her handbag. "Neil, I'm just going to nip down to the High Street before the shops close. Keep an eye on Sarah for me. I won't be long."

"Mum—" Neil protested, but Carole's tall figure was already disappearing out of the hall.

Neil shrugged, and looked round for his little sister. She was waving a brush around, trying to help with the painting but getting more blue paint over herself than on the scenery.

"Mum'll kill me!" Neil groaned as he looked at Sarah's paint-spattered jeans.

He walked down the hall to where the scene painters were at work. Hasheem straightened up, making faces and rubbing his back vigorously.

"Here comes the Puppy Patrol!" he said. "Why aren't you in the pantomime, Neil? There's a dog in it, you know. I didn't think anything could keep you away from dogs."

"You've got to be able to sing," Neil replied. Then he grinned. He was a bit disappointed not to be in the pantomime, but he wasn't going to make a fuss about it.

"And your voice sounds like all the dogs in King Street howling at once." Hasheem chuckled. "That explains a lot."

Neil's parents, Carole and Bob, ran a boarding kennels with a small rescue centre, in the country town of Compton. The thought of all the residents of King Street Kennels howling at once was pretty grim.

Neil looked down. "So what's all this arty stuff, then?"

"It's the road to London," Chris said, squatting back and brushing hair out of his eyes, leaving a blue streak across his forehead. "You know, 'Turn again, Whittington', and all that."

The canvas showed a road and some trees, and blue sky which Chris and Hasheem were filling in. There was a signpost with *London 7* in big black letters.

"Dick makes friends with this stray dog," Chris explained. "In our case with Denny back there." He pointed to a makeshift dressing room at the side of the stage. "Then it goes to London with him and makes his fortune."

Neil wasn't really listening; Emily had been talking about the panto non-stop, and he knew the story backwards. He glanced up at the clock again. Twenty to six. "I'm going to be late," he muttered to himself.

On stage the actors and stagehands had finished moving the furniture around. Gina's older sister, Beth, came out from behind a curtain and stood centre stage. She played Dick Whittington, though she didn't look much like it at present, dressed in blue jeans and a sporty-looking hooded sweatshirt. Her long fair hair was all over the place. Denny trotted on stage as well, and sat at Beth's feet. Everybody else went off, and Neil suddenly became interested as he realized they were going to rehearse one of Denny's scenes.

Beth sat down at the table and pretended to be holding a pen. "Denny, we sold five shillings' worth of spices to Mistress Williams, and three shillings' worth to Master Snip the tailor. Five and three, Denny – what does that come to?"

Denny, who had been listening alertly, barked eight times. Neil, who knew what to look for, saw the hand signal Beth gave him when he had to stop, but it was such a small movement the audience would never notice. They would see a dog that was bright enough to do maths!

Everybody laughed and clapped when the

little scene was finished. Beth stood up and took a bow, then patted Denny. The retriever looked pleased with himself, his tongue hanging out in a wide doggy grin.

"I'm going to teach Fudge to count like that," Sarah announced.

Neil groaned.

At last, the rehearsal was coming to an end. Mr Hamley came down his ladder and Beth led Denny off stage. Everyone else began collecting their belongings and putting on their coats. Gavin Thorpe, the vicar, appeared at the door of the church hall carrying a heavy bunch of keys, ready to lock up.

"At last!" said Neil. "Can we go now?"

"What's the rush?" Hasheem asked. "You've been squirming ever since you got here."

"I've got to get home. Jake's coming tonight."

Hasheem looked puzzled. "You never said you had a mate staying for Christmas."

Chris laughed, and swiped at Hasheem with his brush. "Get real, Hasheem! Since when have you known Neil to be bothered about looking after his friends? Jake's a dog, you dimbo!"

Neil grinned at him. Chris Wilson was his best friend, and he'd heard a lot about Jake in the last few weeks. Jake was a Border collie pup – the son of Neil's beloved dog Sam, and another Border collie called Delilah, who lived at the neighbouring Old Mill Farm. Delilah had a beautiful brood of five adorable pups – and now that Jake was finally old enough to leave his mum, he was coming to live with Neil.

Delilah's owner, Jane Hammond, had promised to bring ten-week-old Jake round at six o'clock that evening. It was one appointment Neil had no intention of missing.

He said goodbye to Chris and Hasheem, and with Sarah in tow went to collect Emily, who was giggling in a corner with her friends, Gina Ward and Julie Baker. She grinned at Neil as he walked towards her.

"I told you Denny's brilliant," she said.

"That's a great scene," Neil agreed, feeling a bit disappointed that he wouldn't be in the show. "You've trained him really well, Gina."

"It's Beth really." Gina went pink with pleasure. "He'll do anything for her."

"This will be the best pantomime ever," Julie said. She laughed. "Do you think we should have Ben in it as well?"

Neil winced. Julie's Old English sheepdog, Ben, was the sloppiest and most loving dog you could hope to meet – and the clumsiest. Neil smiled as he pictured flying props, furniture tipped over and scenery falling on top of a surprised but well-meaning Ben.

Then he stopped smiling. He had noticed the clock again. It said almost five to six – and where was his mother?

It was after six by the time the Parkers set off home in their green Range Rover with the King Street Kennels logo on the side. Neil was fizzing with impatience in the front seat.

"Calm down," Carole told him. "Your dad's at home. Jane will wait for you."

"But I want to be there," Neil said. "Jake's mine. I want to welcome him."

The night was already pitch black and cold and snow had started to fall. Carole was driving carefully for fear of skidding. Snowflakes whirled in the headlights. On the back seat Sarah was bouncing up and down chanting, "I'm going to make a snowman! I'm going to make a snowman!"

"Shut up, Squirt," Neil muttered.

"When are we going to decorate the tree?" Emily asked. "Can we do it tonight? Sarah and I have made some decorations."

"I made a big star," Sarah announced proudly.

"We'll see when we get home," Carole said. "We've got loads to do before Christmas, and this weather isn't helping."

Neil was feeling very excited about the thought of his new puppy. Jake would be his to look after all the time now. It wasn't just fun, Neil knew. It was a big responsibility. Just as well that school had finished, and he would have all the Christmas holiday to settle Jake into his new home.

As the Range Rover approached King Street Kennels, another car, coming from the opposite direction, turned in at the gate. Neil recognized the Hammonds' brown Volvo at once.

"There's Jane!" he exclaimed. "Brill! We haven't missed her!"

As soon as their car had stopped, Neil hurled himself into the drive and over to the Volvo where Jane Hammond was getting out. She was small and slim, with curly dark hair, and she wore a waxed jacket over a thick sweater and cord trousers.

"Hi, Neil," she said, smiling. "All ready for the new arrival?"

"Sure!" Neil grinned back.

Jane opened the back door of the car and reached for a pet carrier on the seat. By this time the rest of the Parkers had joined Neil.

"Is it Jake?" Sarah asked, wriggling past Neil to peer into the back of the Volvo. "Can I see?"

"Let's get him inside," Carole said. "Then we can all see."

"Don't get in the way, Squirt," Neil said. "You're holding things up. Jake will be getting cold."

Jane gave the pet carrier to Neil to carry into the house. He could feel a small body shifting around inside it and hear a scrabbling sound. Against the mesh at the front of the carrier he made out a black nose and two shining eyes.

Light flooded down the steps as the front door opened and the tall, broad-shouldered shape of Bob Parker appeared. "I thought I heard a commotion! Come inside, all of you – it's freezing out here."

Neil hurried inside with the pet carrier, squeezing past his father, and everyone crowded after him down the passage to the kitchen.

Neil set the carrier down in the middle of the kitchen floor. His fingers were shaking as he undid the strap and let the flap fall forward.

"Jake?" His voice was unsteady. "Come out, Jake. This is your new home."

A tiny black muzzle thrust itself out of the shelter of the carrier, followed by the rest of a black and white head with bright eyes and silky ears. Black paws propelled the rest of the puppy a pace or two into the kitchen where he stood watching Neil, who had squatted down in front of him.

"Jake?" Neil repeated. "Hi there, Jake."

The tiny pup looked alertly at the others who stood around him, and back at Neil. He advanced another step and nosed at Neil's outstretched hand. His little tail suddenly began wagging frantically.

"He remembers me!" Neil said delightedly. "He knows who I am." He looked up at Jane, who stood smiling down at him. "Thanks, Jane. This really is going to be the best Christmas ever!"

Chapter Two

Sarah reached out to stroke the puppy, but Carole quickly caught her hand.

"Not just yet," she said. "Give him time to settle in first."

Jake had started to move away from the pet carrier, nose down to the kitchen floor and tail in the air as he tried to make sense of this exciting new place. Neil watched; he knew he had a silly grin on his face, and he didn't care.

"Coffee, Jane?" said Carole, above his head.

"Please. It's arctic out there, isn't it? The snow's already sticking on the lane down to the farm. That's why I was a bit late." She took out an envelope and handed it to Carole. "Before I forget, there's Jake's vaccination certificate.

He'll need a second dose in about a month, but you'll know all about that."

"I've been reading about it," Neil piped up. "If he's not vaccinated, he could get distemper and hepatitis and . . . oh, I've forgotten the others."

"Poor Jake!" said Sarah. "All those needles stuck in him!"

Bob laughed. "No, love, it's all in one injection. Though there is another vaccine against kennel cough. He'd better have that as well, because he's bound to come into contact with the boarding dogs when he's a bit older."

Neil nodded, not taking his eyes off the puppy. Whatever Jake needed to grow into a happy, healthy dog, Neil would see he had it.

As Jake was exploring the kitchen, he came close to the basket where Sam would usually be drowsing at this time. Jake sniffed the blankets inside.

As if on cue, Sam padded into the room, disturbed from his cosy spot in front of the living room fire by the noise everybody was making.

"It's Jake's dad!" Sarah clapped her hands vigorously.

Sam sat beside his basket and watched the young puppy exploring his new surroundings.

"Do you think Sam knows that he's Jake's dad?" Emily asked.

Neil held out his hand to scratch Sam's ears. "I've been reading about that, too," he explained. "Dogs don't really know about families like we do. Wild dogs live in packs, so that's how they think. Sam was here first, so he's pack leader. That means we have to show Jake that Sam's the boss."

"How do we do that?" Emily asked.

"Oh, it's easy. Feed Sam first; pat him and praise him first if they both come to you." He scratched Sam's ears again, smiling affectionately. "Jake's terrific, but Sam mustn't feel left out."

Sam had been Neil's dog for years, ever since he had been found as a puppy, abandoned and wandering on the old Compton railway line. Until recently, he had been a champion in local Agility competitions. But just a few weeks ago, at the same time Jake was born, they had discovered that Sam had a heart murmur. Even though he was still a happy, healthy dog, there would be no more Agility contests for Sam. He had to take it easy from now on.

Neil laughed as Jake put his paws up on the edge of the basket and sniffed curiously at Sam.

Sam bent his head; father and son touched nose to nose.

"Aren't they sweet!" said Emily.

"Hey!" Neil said as Jake's hind feet scrabbled against the basket. The pup was trying to climb in, and Neil wasn't sure how Sam would take the invading of his territory.

Neil gently pushed Jake away. Carefully he picked him up with one hand under his chest and the other supporting his hindquarters, and carried him across the kitchen.

"This is your basket, Jake," he said.

For now, Neil had brought in one of the plastic beds that they used in the rescue centre, and padded it with warm bedding. Puppies always chew their beds, and letting Jake chew a proper basket might hurt him when he was so tiny.

Next to the bed were two big china bowls. Neil put Jake down in front of them and filled one of them with water. Jake stuck his nose in for a long drink.

"Isn't he small?" Sarah said.

"Biggest in the litter!" Neil protested.

"He's very young," Carole explained to Sarah. "But he'll grow. You just wait!"

Sarah gazed at Jake as if she expected him to

18

grow in front of her eyes. "Aren't you going to feed him?" she asked.

"Give him a small meal later on," Jane suggested. "He's on four meals a day at the moment: two of puppy meal with milk, and two of mince mixed with brown bread – cornflakes now and again for a change. I've been putting a teaspoonful of bonemeal and one of cod liver oil in one of the meat meals."

Neil nodded, taking it all in.

"I've brought some of the puppy meal we've been using," Jane went on. "You can change to your own once he's settled in."

Sarah was still watching Jake as he drank. "I'd like a puppy for Christmas," she said.

"You're always wanting a puppy!" laughed Neil.

"You're too young to look after a puppy on your own yet," Carole explained. "But I'm sure Neil would like some help with Jake once he's settled in."

"You're just a pup yourself, Squirt!" said Emily.

Neil didn't say anything.

"Besides," said Bob, "remember that a puppy's for life, not just for Christmas." Every year the Parkers had to find new homes for pups who'd been given as Christmas presents and then abandoned by owners who couldn't cope. People just didn't realize what a responsibility a puppy could be.

As Jake finished his drink Carole said to Neil, "You should really take him outside after that. But it's so cold I've put some newspaper down by the door. Use that for now. Just lift him over there and see if he gets the idea."

Neil did as his mother suggested, but Jake immediately bounced off the newspaper again. Neil put him back. Jake gave him a look as if he wanted to say, "What's all this about?" but after a minute he squatted down and produced the expected puddle.

"Well done, boy! Good dog!" Neil praised him, while Sarah jumped up and down and clapped as if the pup had done something clever. Maybe he had; it was better than in the middle of the floor. All the same, Neil thought, as he collected up the soggy newspaper, he'd be *much* happier when it was warm enough for Jake to go outside.

When Neil went down to breakfast next morning, Jake was romping round the kitchen.

After feeding Sam and then the puppy, he sat down for his own breakfast just as Bob Parker came in through the back door in a swirl of fluffy snow.

"Shut the door, Dad!" cried Emily, already seated at the table. "You're letting the warm air out."

"Yeah, and think of Jake! He'll catch a chill!" Neil warned, pouring himself a bowl of cereal.

The puppy danced around Bob's wellington boots, sniffing the sludgy snow as it fell to the floor and seeming oblivious to the icy blast.

Bob unzipped his thick winter jacket and stomped his feet on the floormat. He nudged Jake back towards his basket. "Sorry, but it's absolutely freezing out there – I had to come inside again for a moment to get warmed up. I've been chipping the ice off the barn doors. They're getting almost impossible to open."

Neil looked up. "Is it that bad?"

"Worst I've seen for a long time. Make sure you've got proper boots on if you go out. The snow is already fairly deep between here and the kennel blocks. I hope it doesn't go on too much longer or we'll have trouble keeping things running."

Emily laughed and pointed towards a pile of

post on the table. "Anyway, if the mail's still being delivered it can't be that bad!"

Neil flicked through the pile. Most of the letters were for Bob and Carole, but there was a copy of the animal magazine that Emily subscribed to, and one large white envelope for him. Neil ripped it open.

"Hey, great," he said. "Look, it's a card from Max and Prince." Quickly he read the few lines scribbled inside the card. "Max says they're recording up here again in the New Year. He might be able to drop in and see us."

Max Hooper, with his dog Prince, was the star of the Parkers' favourite TV programme, *Time Travellers*, and not long ago, Neil and Emily had been extras in an episode recorded at Padsham Castle. Neil and Max had kept in touch ever since, and Neil was delighted at the thought of seeing his friend again. He was sure Max and Prince would love to meet Jake.

Carole had served up eggs and bacon, and was now looking through her own cards.

"One from Mr Bradshaw and Marjorie," she said, passing it over to Bob. "And one from Eddie and Maureen Thomas, and Blackie – look at the paw-print! And a calendar from Preston's – Bob, that reminds me. Did you check up when they'll deliver the dog food I ordered in for the holidays? We'll be needing it before long."

Bob swallowed a mouthful of bacon. "I rang them yesterday. They've got problems fitting in all the deliveries before Christmas, but they promised me it would be here by tomorrow at the latest."

"I'll believe it when I see it," Carole said.

After breakfast, Neil got ready to help with the kennel work.

"Don't forget to wrap up warm," said Carole. "The snow didn't let up overnight."

When Neil opened the back door he saw the courtyard covered with a layer of white, already criss-crossed by lines of footprints from the kennel blocks to the house, the barn, and the separate block that housed the rescue centre. Thin, wispy flakes of snow fluttered down and swirled all round.

Neil pulled down his hat over his ears, and launched himself into the snow.

In the store room he found Kate McGuire, the King Street kennel maid, measuring out the feeds for the boarding dogs. Her fair hair was tied back, and she was wearing some thin thermal gloves.

"Hi!" Neil said. "Jane brought Jake round last night. Are you coming to see him?"

"You bet," Kate said. "Just as soon as I've finished here. This is the last batch." She dug the scoop deep into the sack of biscuits. "We're running low. I hope we get that delivery before Christmas."

"Tomorrow, Dad said," Neil told her. "Do you want me to take these in?" He nodded towards the bowls.

King Street Kennels had two kennel blocks, with the store room between them. Each of the blocks had two rows of ten pens, with an aisle down the middle, and each pen had its own separate exercise run. Today, though, the doors to the runs were closed, to keep out the cold.

As Neil opened the door of Kennel Block Two, a blast of warm air greeted him. The blocks were heated during the colder weather by pipes running through the concrete floor; his dad must have turned the heating right up.

The frantic barking of the last few hungry dogs sank to a contented snuffling as they pushed their noses into their bowls. With the job done, Neil took a few minutes to talk to the dogs. Some of them had been regular visitors to King Street for years.

"Hello there, Bundle," he said, stopping in front of a hairy mongrel who had spent some time in the rescue centre. The last time Bundle was at King Street, he'd been bright pink – the result of a cruel practical joke. "You're looking well."

He slipped Bundle a dog treat from the supply he always carried in his pocket. Next to Bundle was Flora, a Jack Russell who was a regular visitor, and next to her a Welsh corgi called Taffy.

The pen at the far end of the block had been empty when Neil went out the day before. Now it was occupied. Neil peered in to see one of the biggest dogs he'd ever seen, sitting and looking back at him with a sorrowful expression in his liquid brown eyes. The dog had a shaggy brown and white coat, with a white muzzle and chest, and black shading on his face and ears.

"A St Bernard!" Neil exclaimed. "Wow, you're massive, aren't you?" He held out a titbit through the mesh, half afraid that the enormous dog would swallow his fingers as well.

Neil heard Kate's footsteps approaching him down the aisle.

"What's his name, Kate?" asked Neil.

"Bernie. His owner left him here yesterday, while he goes off to Spain for some winter sun." She flicked some snowflakes off her shoulders. "Can't say I blame him."

"But it's warm in here. Anyway, if one of us gets lost in the snow, Bernie can come and find us."

Kate laughed. "Don't bet on it. His owner, John Cartwright, used to train dogs for the

26

mountain rescue service, before he retired. He told me that Bernie was the only dog he'd never been able to train at all."

Neil stared at the St Bernard again. "He's never saved anybody?"

"Not one."

Huh, Neil thought, *I bet I could train him!* Then he stopped himself. He mustn't get too big-headed. John Cartwright was a professional, after all, and if he couldn't train Bernie . . . Neil gave the big dog a last glance as he followed the others out of the kennel block. *All the same*, he thought, *I'd like to have a try*.

As Neil crossed the courtyard again, blowing warm air into his gloved hands, he glanced through the side gate and saw a blue Mini turn into the drive. The car glided silently to a halt on the deepening snow and Gina Ward scrambled out almost before it had stopped. Neil walked over to meet her.

"Hi," he said. "Have you come to—"

He broke off, noticing her tears. "Neil, it's awful!" she said. "We've lost Denny!"

27

Chapter Three

"Lost Denny?" Neil echoed. "What do you mean? How?"

"I don't know." Gina twisted the ends of her scarf worriedly. She looked very upset. "He went out in the garden this morning, and when I went to call him in, he'd gone!"

"Are you sure he isn't hiding?"

While they were talking, Gina's sister Beth had got out of the driver's seat and come to join them.

"Have you seen our garden, Neil?" she asked. "A mouse couldn't hide in there, never mind a dog the size of Denny. I found a loose post in the fence; I think he must have squeezed out that way."

"Have you tried following his paw marks in the snow?" Neil suggested.

Gina shook her head. "It wasn't any good. We could see his prints in the garden, but too many people had been up and down the lane outside." Gina looked up at the white snowflakes drifting down all round them. "Maybe the snow confused him. It's the first time he's seen it settle so deeply. Everything looks so different – even our garden."

"I rang the police," Beth said, "but they haven't heard anything yet. They suggested getting in touch with your dad."

That didn't surprise Neil. Stray dogs in and around Compton often ended up at the King Street rescue centre. Neil had lost count of how many frantic owners the Parkers had reunited with their pets. He knew how Gina and Beth must be feeling but there was nothing he could do to help them – Denny wasn't here.

"I'm sorry," he said, "but we've not heard anything, either."

Beth shook her head. "I didn't expect you would have, really. I know you would have rung us. But we had to give it a try. You will get in touch if he turns up?"

"Of course we will. You'd better come and

give his details to Mum. And let's get inside – it's freezing standing here."

Neil led Beth and Gina to the office. Emily had seen the car from the house, and ran to meet them at the door. She was shocked to hear that Denny was missing.

"What about the pantomime?" she asked. "We can't do it without Denny. He's too important!"

"I know," said Beth. "And he's usually so good. I can't help thinking something horrible has happened."

Carole looked up from her desk. "Don't say that. It's early days yet. Let's not jump to conclusions, eh?" She sat Gina and Beth down in front of the desk and began to record Denny's details for the rescue centre files. Neil and Emily crowded round to listen.

"He was definitely wearing his collar," Gina said. "It has a tag with his name and our phone number. So if someone *has* found him, why haven't they let us know? Only a thief wouldn't call."

"I know this is horrible for you, but you've got to keep calm," Carole said. "He's only been missing two or three hours and it doesn't do any good to think the worst."

Neil exchanged a worried glance with Emily. Denny was such a clever dog, and so well-trained, that if a thief knew about him he might think he could sell him for a good price.

"Have you seen anybody suspicious hanging around?" he asked.

Beth looked blank, and said that as far as she could recall there was nobody in the lane when she let Denny into the garden that morning.

"Tell them about that phone call," said Gina, nudging her sister's arm.

Beth nodded. "Just two or three days ago I had an anonymous phone call. It was a man. He sounded very reasonable at first – asking me lots of questions about the pantomime. Eventually he claimed we were being cruel to Denny by teaching him tricks and making him perform. He asked me not to use him in the show."

"Huh!" Emily snorted. "You don't have to *make* Denny perform. He loves it!"

"What did you say?" Neil asked.

"Nothing. I just put the phone down."

"And did you tell the police?" Carole made a note on the card where she was recording Denny's details.

"No." Beth shrugged. "I thought it was just some crank. But now I wonder whether he came and stole Denny to stop him being in the pantomime."

Everybody was silent for a minute. Neil knew that some trainers were cruel to performing animals, and some kinds of animal were unhappy in captivity, but none of that applied to Denny. He was a happy, healthy dog, and Neil had seen at the rehearsal how he loved to show off. Even so, somebody who didn't know him might think he was rescuing him from ill-treatment.

"I think you should report it to the police now," said Carole.

"Yes, I will." Beth glanced at her watch. "Come on, Gina. Emily, I'll see you later on at rehearsal."

"But will we be doing the pantomime, if Denny can't be found?" Emily protested.

"I don't know. But we can still rehearse. There are lots of scenes that Denny isn't in." She gave Emily a little shake, and managed to smile. "Cheer up, Emily. The show must go on!"

"I've worked out a training programme for Bernie," Neil announced at lunchtime. He sat at the kitchen table, carefully avoiding Jake, who was making little growly rushes at his feet.

"For Bernie?" Bob Parker gave his spaghetti sauce on the cooker a last stir. "I thought you had enough to do, training Jake."

Neil felt himself going red. "Yes, well . . . I thought it would be a surprise for Mr Cartwright."

"John Cartwright has been training dogs for years," Carole pointed out. "If he says Bernie is untrainable . . ."

"But there's no harm in trying," Neil said. "Em, you'll help me, won't you?"

Emily sat down, and pushed her untidy dark hair out of her eyes.

"Not now. I've got a rehearsal. If I've got time later I might give you a hand."

"Sarah?" Asking for his little sister's help was a last resort for Neil – but probably better than nothing.

"I'm going to build a snowman!" Sarah said. "Fudge is going to help me."

"Thanks a bunch," Neil muttered. He was beginning to think that his attempt at training Bernie would have to wait.

"It's too cold for Fudge to be outside," Carole said, as she began serving out the sauce. "But

Neil's very good at building snowmen." She gave Neil a hard look. "Aren't you, Neil?"

Neil shrugged. "Oh, sure."

Bob chuckled. "And don't be too disappointed if Bernie doesn't co-operate when you do get a chance to take him out. I don't think snow and Bernie get along very well together!"

When Emily had gone to her rehearsal, Neil helped Sarah to build a snowman in the courtyard during a break in the weather. He rolled a huge snowball for the body while Sarah made a smaller one for the head. She fetched an old hat and a scarf, while Neil raided the storeroom for biscuits to make eyes, a nose and mouth.

Neil bent down and plunged his hand deep into a large, brown sack. Scrabbling round at the bottom, he pulled out a handful of dog biscuits and stuffed them in his jacket pocket. On his way out, he noticed that they really were getting low on dog food – there was probably only enough to last a couple of days.

When he went back into the courtyard he found Sarah rolling a third snowball.

"Not another snowman!" he protested. "I'm

freezing. And it's getting harder to walk in this stuff!" Neil kicked out at a lump of snow on the ground.

"No, stupid," Sarah said. "This is a snow dog!"

They finished off the snow dog with a curved twig for a tail and Sarah's scarf around its neck. She didn't want it getting cold. It didn't look like any breed of dog Neil had ever seen. Just as they had completed their snow sculpture, it started to snow again, big wet flakes that settled on the window ledge and the ground and the roofs of the kennel blocks. They had to leave the snowman and his dog, and take shelter. If the snow got much deeper, Neil thought, they might get cut off for Christmas.

As Neil went into the kitchen, something tiny collided with his foot. He looked down to see Jake trying to attack his boot. Jake was into feet. If you were that small, Neil thought, feet might be the most important thing you could see.

Grinning, he squatted down and tickled the little black and white pup on the tummy. "What about some training, Jake?"

Neil started by calling Sam over from his

basket. The Border collie came promptly and stood looking at Neil with an alert expression.

"Now watch this," Neil said to Jake. He took out a dog treat, showed it to Sam, and said, "Sit!" Sam sat at once; Neil gave him the treat and praised him. "Now, Jake, do you think you can do that?"

Jake had watched with an interested look in his bright eyes, but as soon as Neil took out another titbit he started bouncing around, trying to reach his hand.

"No!" said Neil.

He held out the dog treat to Jake, who sniffed it while his little tail wagged excitedly. Neil lifted the titbit above his head, and Jake sat down to keep his eyes on it more easily. He gave Jake the titbit and fondled his ears as the puppy wolfed it down.

Looking at Jake, Neil thought about Beth and Gina, who must have been missing Denny desperately. He wished he could do something to help. It would be a miserable Christmas for the Ward family without Denny.

Chapter Four

Neil knew how right he was when his dad brought Emily back from rehearsal. She was almost in tears.

"It was awful. Everybody was upset, trying to work without Denny. And Gina's really worried because Denny might freeze to death if he's out all night in this snow."

"It almost makes you hope he has been stolen," Bob said, taking his coat off. "At least a thief would keep him inside. It'll be bitter outside tonight. If the snow keeps lying like it has been doing I can see problems ahead."

He shook the melting remains of snow off his coat. Jake flinched and his paws skittered on the floor as one of the flying drops hit him.

"Hey Dad!" Neil protested, scooping Jake up.

"Sorry, little fellow." Bob grinned and rubbed Jake's muzzle with one finger. "Didn't see you down there."

"Maybe one of the dogs could track Denny," Emily suggested, cheering up a bit. "Perhaps Bernie could do it."

"Not yet – I haven't worked my magic on him!"

"Modesty is not your strong point, is it?" Emily tried to hide a smile. "I think Jake could do a better job of tracking than Bernie."

Bob was still stroking the pup in Neil's arms. "Somehow I don't think so." He smiled gently down at Jake. "He's got a lot of learning to do first."

Just then Carole and Kate opened the back door and bustled into the warmth of the kitchen. Carole's hands were filled with holly, covered in shiny scarlet berries. She laid it carefully on the table, then unwound her scarf and pulled off her woolly hat.

"It's cold enough out there to freeze your feet off," she said. "Is there a hot drink on offer, Bob?"

Bob hurriedly went to the sink to fill the kettle. Kate stripped off her gloves and blew on fingers turned pink with cold.

"It's at times like this," she said, "that I fancy a job in a nice, warm office."

"No!" Emily protested. "You can't!"

Kate laughed. "I was only joking. I don't really. But the snow's getting worse. We'll need skis to get across the courtyard tomorrow."

Neil looked out of the window again. A white veil of snowflakes whirled against the darkening sky.

"Maybe we'll be snowed in," he suggested. "That would be ace!"

His mother gave him one of her looks. "If we are, you'll soon be wishing I'd shopped for more food. Feeding you lot is like feeding an army on the march. Not to mention the dogs!"

Bob poured coffee into mugs and handed one to Kate. "You're never going to be able to ride your bike home in this."

Kate wrapped her hands gratefully round the steaming mug. "No need to worry. Glen said he would collect me."

"Good," said Bob. "And I really don't think you should try to come in tomorrow."

"But the dogs still have to be looked after," Kate objected. "It's harder work when the weather's like this."

Bob shrugged. "We'll cope. But if it keeps on

snowing, you might not be able to get here. And if you do, you might not be able to get home again. That would really mess up your plans for Christmas."

"What are you doing for Christmas, Kate?" Emily asked.

"Spending it with Glen, of course," said Neil, grinning. "Look, she's gone bright red!"

"Neil!" said his mother.

Just then the doorbell rang. Emily went to answer it, and came back with Kate's boyfriend, Glen Paget, his collar turned up and his long, fair hair plastered to his head with melting snow. He said hello to everyone, and scratched Jake behind the ears. "Hi there, midget. I've heard a lot about you."

"Listen, Glen," Carole said, "tell Kate that she's not to try coming into work tomorrow. The snow's getting worse. It's not worth risking an accident."

"She's right, you know," Glen said to Kate. "It was hard enough getting here tonight."

Kate looked from Carole to Bob, and then back at Glen. Reluctantly, she nodded. "All right."

"And don't look so guilty," Bob told her. "Have an extra day's holiday on the Puppy Patrol."

"And this," added Carole, taking a parcel in shiny paper out of a cupboard and presenting it to Kate.

Kate hugged it to her and thanked them. "I'm really sorry. I just hope you have a good Christmas."

"We will," Bob said. "And you enjoy yours, too."

"I'll make sure she does," Glen promised cheerfully.

As Kate and Glen were about to leave, Neil thought about Denny. Glen was involved with an Animal Rights group, and he might be able to shed some light on the crank phone call Beth had received.

"Glen," he asked, "do you know the Wards' dog, Denny?"

Glen shook his head. Quickly Neil explained about Denny's cleverness, and how someone had phoned to tell Beth she was cruel to make the dog perform. "And now Denny's missing," he finished. "Do you know of anyone who might have taken him?"

"To keep him out of the pantomime?" Glen thought for a minute. "That's a tough one, Neil. Some people don't like to see performing animals, but a trained pet dog is different from lions and tigers that should be in the wild. I can tell you this, nobody in my group would steal a dog. I doubt that it's anything to do with Animal Rights."

"It doesn't sound as if Denny was stolen," Neil said when Glen and Kate had gone. He almost felt disappointed. At least an Animal Rights group would look after Denny.

"So he might be wandering about in the snow," said Emily, gloomy again. "And they've cancelled tomorrow's rehearsal. If someone doesn't find Denny soon, there won't be any pantomime."

In the excitement of Jake's arrival the night before, they'd forgotten the Christmas tree. Neil, Emily and Sarah decorated it in the sitting room after supper. Sarah insisted on Bob lifting her up so that she could put the glittery star she had made on the topmost branch. Carole kept the fragile baubles out of Jake's reach, but the excitable little puppy still managed to roll himself up in tinsel.

"He's so sweet!" said Emily.

Carole was on her knees disguising the very ordinary bucket that held the tree with shiny Christmas paper. She stopped what she was doing to unwind Jake.

43

"You'll have to keep an eye on him, Neil," she said. "I hate to think what he would do if you left him in here by himself."

"Sure, Mum." Neil grinned, and scooped Jake up to pick the last strand of tinsel out of his glossy coat. "Behave yourself, Jake, do you hear? And make sure you don't scare Father Christmas!"

"I think we should write to Father Christmas and ask him to bring Denny back," Sarah announced.

"You've left it a bit late," Emily said.

"Well, I'm going to!"

"You write if you want to, love," Carole said. "The Wards couldn't hope for a better Christmas present, that's for sure."

*

On Christmas Eve morning Neil woke early. He looked out to see the courtyard and the roofs of the kennel blocks covered with snow. There had been another heavy snowfall during the night, but now only a few flakes were drifting slowly down. The bedroom window was covered with frost patterns, and icicles hung from the gutter above.

The rest of the house was quiet. It would be a good time for a training session with Bernie. Neil would have to manage without a helper, but at least there would be no one there to laugh at him.

He washed quickly, and dragged on jeans and a couple of thick sweaters, wondering what he could use to lay a trail of scent for Bernie. Then he had an idea.

He took the pillowcase from his pillow, fished out some abandoned socks from under the bed and put them in the case, then topped it up with a couple of his shirts, a sweater and some more socks from the laundry basket. That lot should have plenty of his scent on them. Satisfied, he tied a knot in the top of the pillowcase and crept downstairs.

When he got down to the kitchen, Jake was asleep, but Sam lifted his head alertly from his basket.

"No, Sam," Neil said. "Not now. It's far too cold for you outside."

When he had put on his boots and padded jacket, Neil took his bundle outside into the exercise field. On one side of the field the powdery snow had drifted so that it came almost to the top of his boots, and his breath made a cloud in the icy morning air. Starting near the gate, he dragged the bundle through the snow where it wasn't too deep, back and forth for a long way, and finally buried it.

"Right," he said to himself. "Let's see what he makes of that."

Neil opened the door of Kennel Block Two a crack, and slid quietly inside. He didn't want to wake all the dogs; the racket would wake everyone else, and his mum and dad would be furious.

The air inside the block was warm, and the dogs were mostly still asleep. One or two raised their heads drowsily and watched Neil as he padded along the aisle between the pens.

When he reached Bernie's pen, Neil took the lead from the hook outside the door and went in. Bernie was snoring in a regular rumble that shook his whole body. Neil bent down and tugged at his collar.

"Come on, boy! Wake up!"

Bernie opened one liquid eye and closed it again. His snores died away into a kind of hiccup, and then started up again. Neil gave him a gentle shove.

"Come *on!*"

This time Bernie woke up properly, thrust himself to his feet and gave himself a shake. Neil grinned and slipped him a dog treat.

"That's better. Let's go, Bernie!"

As Neil led Bernie outside he heard a high-pitched yapping from the Pomeranian in the nearest pen, and Bundle's deeper bark answering it from further down the row. *Go back to sleep*, he willed them silently, leading Bernie at a trot down the garden path and through the gate.

Once in the exercise field, Neil forgot about the other dogs. Pulling out one of his socks that he'd stashed in his pocket, Neil waved it under Bernie's nostrils. The dog's nostrils flared as he sniffed it. Neil then unclipped Bernie's lead and let him nose around in the snow, trying to encourage him to find the end of the scent trail he had laid.

When Bernie reached it, he became quite excited, snuffling around with his nose in Neil's footprints.

Neil crouched down beside him. "Seek, Bernie!"

Bernie nosed around again, and at last came back to Neil and planted a huge, snow-covered paw on his chest. Neil staggered back, laughing.

"No, you daft dog! Other end . . . seek!"

Somehow, Bernie seemed to grasp the idea. He plodded back and forth along the scent trail, until he reached the pillowcase that Neil had buried, and scraped energetically at the snow to uncover it.

Neil stooped over him and gave him a big hug. "Brill, Bernie! Well done!"

He fed Bernie a couple of dog treats, and decided he would end the training session there. Next time, Bernie would remember he had done well. If I play with him for a bit, Neil thought, he'll want to try again.

They had ended up near the clump of bushes at the far end of the field. Neil found a stick, and threw it for Bernie. The huge dog lolloped back and forth, scattering snow everywhere, enjoying the game just as if he were a pup like Jake.

Neil only remembered the time when snow started to fall again. It soon came down in multiple sheets of tingly, wet drops and Neil quickly called Bernie back to him.

"Breakfast, Bernie?"

He was sure the St Bernard grinned at him. He clipped on the lead again and tried to lead him away but instead Bernie sat rock-like, and gave a yawn. Neil tugged the lead gently, and when Bernie still did not respond he hauled on the St Bernard's collar. It was like trying to shift a cart-horse. "Up, Bernie! Come on! Just for me?" Neil beamed at the dog. "Please?"

At last Bernie heaved himself to his feet and trundled off up the field, with Neil striding alongside him, picking up the pillowcase as he went. As soon as Bernie reached the gate, he flopped to the ground again.

Neil swung open the gate and motioned for Bernie to go through.

Bernie dropped his nose to his paws looking completely uninterested.

"I don't often beg, Bernie, but will you please come back to the kennels with me? The snow is going down my neck!"

The St Bernard's head swivelled to look at Neil, and then with a ripple of muscles he rose and plodded back towards the kennels. Already the snow was so heavy that he could hardly see the shape of the house and the kennel blocks, but as he drew closer, he could make out the figure of his father coming towards him across the courtyard. Neil broke into a run, with Bernie alongside him.

"Dad!" he panted, as he reached him. "You'll never guess what Bernie . . ."

His voice died away as he saw his father's face. Bob Parker was hardly ever angry, but he looked angry now.

"Neil," he said, "what exactly have you been doing?"

Chapter Five

"Sorry?" Neil said, staring up into his father's face.

"I hope you are." Bob still sounded grim. He motioned for Neil to follow him across the courtyard. "Your mother and I were woken up at some unearthly hour by all the dogs barking their heads off—"

"Oops," said Neil.

"When we found out that Bernie was missing from his pen, the first thing we thought was that somebody must have broken into the kennels. Then your mother looked into your room, and found you were missing as well."

"I'm sorry, Dad. I just thought it was a good chance to give Bernie a bit of training. And he—"

"You didn't think at all," Bob interrupted. He stopped as they came to the door of Kennel Block One; when he spoke again he sounded less angry. "Neil, I know you meant it for the best. But your mum and I have got enough to do today, especially when Kate isn't here, without having to look for a missing dog that isn't missing at all. I was within a couple of minutes of ringing the police. Go and put Bernie back in his pen right now. And Neil . . . try to be a bit more sensible in future."

When Neil had kennelled Bernie he went back to the house and found the rest of the family having breakfast round the kitchen table. Sam and Jake were both looking on hopefully. Neil stamped snow off his boots.

"That smells good," he said, sniffing appreciatively as Carole dished up sausages and bacon.

"Think yourself lucky that I didn't give yours to Jake," Carole said. "Sit down and . . . Neil – what in the world is *that*?"

Neil was still carrying the pillowcase full of clothes that he had used to lay the scent trail for Bernie.

"It's just clothes and stuff," he explained. "I used it to—"

"If you ask me, you've been playing football with it!" Carol said. "Neil, just look at it! That was a good pillowcase."

Neil looked at his bundle properly for the first time since Bernie had dug it up. He had to admit it was filthy, and it had got torn a bit. Still, in Neil's view, it was worth it if it had helped to train Bernie.

"You see, Mum—"

"I don't want to know." Carole sounded exasperated. "I really don't. Just take it up to the laundry basket, and then come and have your breakfast."

The snow went on falling. By the time breakfast was over, the footprints Neil and his dad had made in the courtyard were filled in again.

"I'm glad I finished the Christmas shopping," Carole said, as she cleared the table. "I wouldn't fancy driving in this."

Bob got up, nodding at Neil and Emily. "Come on, you two. Feeding time."

Without Kate, it took longer than usual to make up the feeds for the boarding dogs. Bob measured out the different diets, while Neil and

Emily transported the bowls of food and water to the two kennel blocks and the rescue centre. Carole stayed indoors to get on with Christmas preparations.

"To think I ever wanted snow!" Neil groaned, slipping and narrowly saving the food bowl he was carrying. Even in gloves his fingers felt like icicles. The falling snow was so intense he could hardly see across the courtyard. He couldn't help wondering what would happen to Denny, if he was out in this. There had been no word from Beth or Gina since the day before and Neil could imagine how they must be feeling.

When the feeding was done, Neil and Emily went back into the kitchen, where Carole had hot drinks ready. A tray of mince pies had appeared on the kitchen table. Neil reached for one.

"Hands off!" Carole swatted him. "They're for tomorrow."

"Quality control, Mum," Neil protested.

To avoid any more arguments, Carole put a packet of chocolate biscuits on the table. "Is there any sign of the dog food?" she asked Bob.

"No. I'm starting to wonder if the delivery van will be able to get through. I'm going to give

Preston's a ring." Bob drained his mug and went out into the hall.

Emily said, "Is there any news of Denny?"

Carole shook her head. "I'd have told you if there was. Try not to worry, love. He might have found shelter somewhere."

She meant to be comforting, but she still sounded anxious. Everybody knew the danger Denny was in. Even watching Jake's antics as he tried to chase his own tail couldn't cheer Neil up. And he couldn't think of anything more that they could do.

When Bob came back, he was looking worried as well, but for a different reason.

"I got through to the delivery manager, and he told me the snow had messed up all their schedules. Only to be expected, I suppose. He said he'd try to get a van through to us, but he couldn't promise."

"Well," Carole said, "we've food for a couple of days. Let's see . . ." She started counting on her fingers. "Today's Thursday. Christmas Day and Boxing Day . . . Bob, if they don't deliver today, there won't be another delivery until next Monday."

"What are we going to do?" asked Neil.

"There's the Cash and Carry on the other side

of Compton," Carole said. "It'll be expensive but we could buy some cases of tinned dog food there, and biscuits."

"Getting there's the problem," said Bob. He straightened up. "Let's leave it until lunch time. Then we'll decide. Neil, come and help me clear the drive so we can get the car out, and if the Preston's van arrives, it can get in."

By the end of the morning, Neil's back was aching from shovelling snow and he was sweating inside his padded jacket. More snow was falling all the time, so he couldn't help feeling that all his efforts would be wasted. But he and his father had cleared a path from the road to the house, and Bob had put down some of the straw that was used for the dogs' bedding, to help wheels get a grip.

"If the snow stops," Bob said, "we'll clear some of the exercise runs. That way the dogs can get out for a bit."

"Fantastic," Neil grunted. He never wanted to see another spade for the rest of his life. "Can we go in now? I've still got to wrap presents."

"Better do it later," Bob suggested. "When Sarah's in bed. She won't give you a minute's peace, otherwise."

Neil grinned.

Neil and Bob took the spades back to the store room. On the way, they met Emily and Sarah, plodding back through the snow from the rescue centre.

"We've been checking up on the dogs," Emily explained. "They're really restless because they haven't been out. We played with them for a bit but Sarah wanted to play with Jake."

"Look for her Christmas presents, more like," Neil smirked.

"We'll try to get them out this afternoon," Bob promised. "Otherwise there'll be a lot of very messy pens to clean out."

Emily made a face. "There already are!"

Carole was in the store room when Neil and Bob put away the spades.

"I've made a list," she explained, waving it. "Of what we really can't do without. If Preston's don't turn up, I'll go to the Cash and Carry after lunch."

Mention of lunch reminded Neil that he was starving. He led the way across the courtyard to the house. Halfway there, he was met by Sam, padding through the snow and waving his tail cheerfully.

"Oh, Sam!" Neil exclaimed. "Don't say you've

learnt how to open the back door!"

He was leading Sam back indoors when a dreadful thought struck him. Where was Jake? He hurried on ahead into the kitchen. It was empty. Though Neil looked under the table and in the spaces behind the fridge and the cooker, there was no sign of the vulnerable little puppy.

Neil dashed out into the passage.

"Jake! Jake!" he called anxiously into the emptiness.

No little puppy scurried up to answer him. Everything was quiet. Neil quickly checked the sitting room, the dining room they hardly ever used, the cloakroom and the cupboard under the stairs. Nothing. Emily tried to ask him what he was up to but he rushed past her into the kitchen without answering.

"Jake! Jake, where are you?"

Carole caught up with Neil first. She took one look at his panic-stricken face and asked, "Neil! What on earth is wrong?"

"Mum! Dad!" Neil gasped out frantically, resisting their efforts to calm him. "Jake's missing. I can't find him anywhere!"

Chapter Six

"Steady on," Bob said. "He must be around here somewhere."

"I've looked," Neil said. "He must have got out. I think Sam opened the back door."

"I doubt even Sam's clever enough for that," said Carole. "But one of us might not have shut it properly."

"Jake loves exploring," Emily said worriedly.

Neil headed for the door. "He'll freeze out there!"

"Hang on," said Bob. "Let's make sure he isn't here, first."

"I said, I've looked."

"So let's look again."

Neil felt frustrated at the methodical way his father started checking the downstairs rooms again, and then went upstairs, even though Jake hadn't learnt to climb stairs yet.

Neil ran outside into the courtyard with Emily. He looked at the ground to see if he could find pawprints leading away from the back door – but a busy morning of people tramping back and forth through the snow made it difficult to see anything clearly. Any marks there were which might have been tiny pawprints were rapidly filling up with snow. It was useless.

"Where do you think he'd go?" Emily asked.

"I don't know. He's not really been out yet. He hasn't got any favourite places."

Neil and Emily began to search the courtyard, calling for Jake all the time. Neil was frightened that the puppy might have got out onto the road, but he realized that was unlikely. He would have seen Jake if the pup had come out while he and his father were shovelling snow in the drive, and they had closed the side gate carefully when they had finished.

The doors of the kennel blocks and the rescue centre were all firmly closed to keep the heat in. Red's Barn was closed as well, but Bob had been in and out fetching straw, and Jake could have slipped in then. Neil and Emily searched.

The barn was a wonderful place for a little dog to play and hide, but after a few minutes they were sure Jake was not there either.

When they left the barn they saw Bob coming out into the courtyard. "Any luck?" he called over to them.

"No," said Neil. "Let's try the garden."

All the while Neil was trying to push down the sick feeling in his stomach, desperately hoping that he would see the little black and white Border collie come bounding towards him through the snow. He wondered how long Jake had been outside. He would freeze to death if they didn't find him soon.

There was still no sign of Jake when he and Bob and Emily came to the field gate. Through the swirling snow Neil could just make out the hedge that separated their land from the Hammonds'.

"Do you think Jake tried to go home?" he asked Bob.

"To Old Mill Farm? I doubt it. Jane delivered him here by road. He wouldn't know the way across the fields."

"We could ring Jane, though," Neil suggested.

"She'll ring us if Jake turns up. I don't want to worry her. Not yet, anyway."

Emily pushed open the gate into the field. "He could have come through here. Sam used to get through the hedge when he went to visit Delilah. Let's start looking."

Neil bit back a groan. The field was huge! If Jake was wandering round, they could easily miss him in the snow. The idea crossed his mind that he might get Bernie to track Jake, but he had to face up to the fact that he hadn't made any real progress with the dopey St Bernard. Not enough to risk Jake's life to his tracking skills.

Neil started calling again, working his way alongside the hedge, poking into the bushes with a stick to see if Jake was hiding. Snow spattered from the branches to the ground as he disturbed them, but there was no Jake.

Eventually he reached the clump of trees and bushes at the far end of the field.

"Jake! Jake!"

For a few seconds he heard nothing except his own panting breath. Then he thought that he could make out a faint whimpering. Emily came pounding up, skidded to a halt beside him and grabbed his arm.

"Call again."

"Jake!"

This time Neil was certain. Jake had answered him. He plunged into the undergrowth, dislodging great masses of snow that slithered wetly onto his shoulders. Neil didn't notice. As he called Jake, the pup's reply had become a feeble yapping.

Neil found him at last in front of a huge clump of brambles several feet from the fence. Trailing stems arched over, interlaced so they protected the ground underneath from some of the snow. He pushed back the curtain with one gloved hand. Beneath it, Jake was crouched on a carpet of snow and dead leaves. When Neil appeared he got up, staggered a couple of paces to sniff Neil's hand, and then collapsed again, shivering. Neil gathered him up.

"Oh, Jake!" He was swallowing tears; he told himself that was stupid, now that Jake was found. "Jake, you daft dog. What have you been up to?"

Back in the kitchen, Neil wrapped Jake in a blanket and settled him in his basket in a warm spot by the cooker. He was still limp and shivering. Carole quickly heated some milk for him.

Moments later, Neil was crouching down beside Jake and offering him the bowl of warm milk. The puppy lapped feebly at it and then closed his eyes.

"He's ill," Neil said anxiously.

"He just needs to warm up," Carole said. "Come away. Let him rest for a bit."

Neil tried to carry on helping his parents with the kennel work but he was finally overcome with distraction.

Looking in on him for the umpteenth time, Neil was still worried. Jake wasn't properly asleep. He kept twitching and whimpering, and he didn't want his milk.

Neil dragged his father back into the kitchen for a second opinion. "I think we should take him to see Mike," Neil said.

Mike Turner took care of all the dogs in King Street Kennels. Neil knew that if there was anything seriously wrong with Jake he couldn't be in better hands.

"Mike might not be at the surgery," Bob said. "It's Christmas Eve. And it'll be difficult to get there in this."

"It's stopped snowing," Carole said, over-hearing their conversation as she stepped inside. "And the Preston's van hasn't turned up yet. If Mike is there, I could go to the Cash and Carry and take Jake on the same trip."

Bob nodded. It was probably best to make sure the pup hadn't caught anything serious.

Carole went out into the hall to telephone the vet.

Neil crouched anxiously over Jake, stroking his silky head. Sam came close and nosed his son, almost as if he was worrying as well.

"Mike's at the surgery," Carole said as she came back into the room. "He'll see Jake if we go right away. He was just about to leave for the holidays – I only just caught him. Emily, you'd better come with me and hold Jake on your lap."

Neil stood up. "Why can't I go? Jake's my dog."

"Because you'll be more help here," Carole said.

"Your mother's right," Bob added, before Neil could protest again. "I need you here. If the Preston's van turns up, you'll have to help me carry boxes. There's still paths to clear, and the runs, and—"

"But I've shovelled snow all morning," Neil muttered rebelliously. "It's not fair."

"Neil," Bob said, "we had enough trouble from you first thing this morning. Don't start being difficult now. Besides, which is more important, getting Jake to the vet quickly or standing here arguing?"

"I know . . ." It was hard for Neil to admit his dad was right. "You'd better look after him," he said to Emily, as she slipped into her winter coat.

"Of course I will," she said sympathetically, swathing Jake in a blanket from his basket so that only his nose poked out of the folds. "I promise, Neil."

When Carole and Emily had gone, Bob let Neil take the dogs one or two at a time into the barn for some play and exercise, while he cleaned out the pens. It was just the sort of job Neil liked, and at any other time he would have enjoyed himself. Now he was just worried about Jake, and wishing he could have gone with him instead of Emily. Sarah, however, was quite happy singing Christmas songs to the dogs.

"Time for a break," Bob said, as he collected the last two dogs from Kennel Block One. "No sign of the Preston's van yet."

As Neil followed his father from the barn, the snow was falling again and refused to give up its relentless deluge of King Street Kennels and the Compton area. Huge feathery flakes were already piling up over ground they had cleared that morning. The Range Rover's tracks from just a couple of hours before were already invisible. Sarah, clasping her dad's hand, was having trouble tripping her way through the deep blanket of snow.

"Mum's not back yet," Neil said.

Bob glanced at his watch. "She's been gone long enough." He frowned, and added thoughtfully, "Quite long enough to see Mike and then go on to the Cash and Carry. The snow must be holding her up."

"Or maybe there's something really bad

wrong with Jake!" Neil said, panicky all over again.

"I doubt it," Bob said, reassuring him. He pushed open the kitchen door and Neil followed him inside, shaking snow off himself. "If you're really worried," his dad went on, "I'll try giving Mike a ring."

With Neil at his heels, he went out to the telephone in the passage and dialled the surgery number. Neil could just hear the faint ringing; it went on and on, until the answering machine cut in. Starting to feel desperate, Neil said, "Where is he?"

"The message says they're closed now until Monday," Bob said, starting to dial another number. "Which suggests that your mum made it to the surgery. Mike wouldn't have left when he knew she was coming. I'll try him on his mobile."

He gave a nod to Neil as this time someone answered the call. "Hello . . . Mike?"

Neil could hear the speaker at the other end, but not the words he was saying. He shifted restlessly from foot to foot and tried to make sense of his dad's end of the conversation.

"They did . . . Great. And Jake? Yes . . . yes, I see. Fine." He stuck a thumb up and grinned at

Neil. Neil felt suddenly shaky with relief. "And they left when? Oh . . . no, she was going to the Cash and Carry, for dog food. Yes, I know . . . yes. It was?" Bob listened for a long time and then said, "OK, Mike, thanks. It's probably nothing to worry about. Cheerio . . . and Happy Christmas."

He put the phone down, frowning again.

"How's Jake?" Neil asked anxiously.

"Oh, Jake's fine. Mike says he was starting to perk up already by the time he got to the surgery. He was exhausted more than anything else. He just needs rest and warmth."

Neil felt a big grin spread over his face. "That's great!"

"Mike closed the surgery as soon as your mum left. He went home, and he tells me the snow ploughs had been out on the main Compton to Padsham road, so he didn't have much trouble getting there."

"Then where's Mum?" Neil asked. "Why hasn't she brought Jake home?"

"That's what I'd like to know," said Bob. "She's had plenty of time to get to the Cash and Carry. So where are they now?"

Chapter Seven

Neil and Bob stood in the passage staring at each other. Then Bob shook himself.

"I'm losing my mind," he said, slapping his forehead. "Your mum took the mobile phone with her. I can call her on that."

He picked up the phone again and dialled a number.

Neil bit his lip.

Bob started to shake his head. "Nope. 'Fraid I'm getting a number unobtainable message. The battery must have run out."

"So what do we do now?"

"Listen, Neil, I'm going to get on outside. There's nothing we *can* do stuck here. You stay near a phone, and give me a shout if your mum calls."

"And what if she doesn't?"

Bob frowned, and tugged at his beard. "We'll worry about that later. Come on, Sarah, are you going to help me out again?"

When his father and Sarah had gone outside, Neil went back to the kitchen. After all the worry about Jake, he realized that he was starving again. He pulled off his jacket and boots, poured himself some milk, and made a jam sandwich. Then he gave Sam a couple of dog biscuits. Sitting at the table, he ruffled the Border collie's fur.

"They'll be back soon, Sam," he said. "Everything'll be fine. You'll see."

Sam looked up at him, his eyes bright and trusting. Neil hoped that he was telling him the truth.

He hadn't been waiting in the kitchen long when Sarah skipped in, singing *Jingle Bells*. The trouble was, she only knew the first line. You could have too much of anything.

"Do you have to?" Neil said in mock exasperation.

Sarah gave him a black look. "Don't be so rude. Jingle bells, jingle bells, jingle all—" She broke off as if a thought had struck her. "Neil, will Father Christmas be able to get here, through all this snow?"

Neil sighed. "He drives a sledge."

Sarah thought about this for a moment, and a beaming smile spread over her face. "That's all right, then. Cos I wrote to him and asked him to bring Denny back for Beth and Gina."

"He might not be able—"

"Yes, he will! Father Christmas is magic. He can do anything. Jingle bells, jingle bells . . ."

To Neil's relief, his little sister skipped off again, back outside to help Bob. Probably driving him mad with *Jingle Bells*, Neil thought. All the same, he wished she wasn't so confident. Her Christmas would be spoilt if Denny still wasn't found.

Sarah's footsteps had hardly died away when the phone rang. Neil shot out into the passage.

"King Street Kennels."

At first all he could hear was crackling. He raised his voice. "Hello . . . hello? I can't hear you."

Then words started to come through.

"Neil, it's Mum—"

Through the interference Neil could hardly recognize her voice.

"Listen, we're—"

"What was that?"

". . . battery's running out. We're—"

Neil gritted his teeth in frustration as the voice was drowned out in another wash of crackling. When it came back his mum was saying, ". . . over the bridge and up the hill. Have you got that, Neil?"

"No!" Neil was starting to panic. "I didn't hear the first bit. Where are you?"

Carole's voice came again, obviously

shouting, but sounding hardly any louder. "Can't get back . . . Emily's hurt, she—" More crackling. ". . . to help Jake."

"Jake?" Neil repeated, more alarmed than ever. "What about Jake? What's wrong?"

This time nothing but the crackling noise replied. The connection went dead.

He put down the phone and then tried ringing his mother's mobile phone number.

It was still unobtainable.

Giving up at last, he went outside to find his father.

Bob had no more success than Neil at getting through to the mobile phone.

"She said Emily was hurt!" Neil kept repeating. "And something's the matter with Jake. She said something about helping Jake!"

He couldn't stop trying to make sense of the few scraps of news that had come through. "What are we going to do?"

Bob took a deep breath. "I'm going to ring the police."

"But we don't even know where Mum is!"

"They can put out a call to all cars to look out for her. That's more than we can do, stuck here without transport." He started to dial again.

"Take it easy, Neil. Panicking won't help. In this sort of weather, a few cars are bound to get stuck here and there."

Neil couldn't bear to go on listening. He went back into the kitchen. The few words of his mum's phone call kept churning around in his mind. If only the battery hadn't failed! There was a spare in the office. She should have taken it with her.

Then Neil started to think. If his mum was stuck, if Emily was hurt and something – Neil didn't let himself wonder what – had happened to Jake, she might not be able to leave them to get to a proper phone. What could he do to help her? If someone took them the spare battery, then Carole could call the police, or an ambulance, or a breakdown service for the car, or whatever she wanted. But there wasn't anyone to do it. Except me, Neil thought. And I don't know where she is.

He considered the garbled phone call again. His mum had said, ". . . over the bridge and up the hill."

The Cash and Carry was over the other side of Compton, across the river and about as far as it could be from King Street Kennels. The route Carole would have taken was well used, and if she was stuck there she could easily have found someone to give them a lift or take a message. But she hadn't, so they were somewhere else. Carole must have had a reason to turn off the main road. Neil's mind was racing with possibilities.

On this side of the river was a whole maze of minor roads and lanes, leading over the hills and dropping down again to rejoin the main road on the King Street side of town. What Neil's mum had said would fit if she was up there somewhere. Neil swallowed, and clenched his fists.

"I'm going to do it!" he said aloud.

Just then Bob came into the kitchen; Neil wondered if he'd heard, but all he said was, "Stay by the phone, Neil", and went outside.

Feeling like a thief, Neil crept down the passage to the office and slid the spare phone battery into his pocket. As he was putting his jacket and boots on again, Sam came padding up to him. His head was cocked and his tail waved hopefully. Neil stooped and patted him.

"Poor old boy, you've been stuck inside for ages. But you can't—"

He broke off, and poked his head outside the back door. Since he had been indoors the snow had stopped completely. A pale, watery sun had broken through the cloud, and the surface of the snow glittered faintly. Neil thought it wasn't as cold as it had been. He went back to Sam.

"OK, boy, why not?" he said. "It's not so bad out there now, and you could do with a walk." Sam needed his exercise like all the other dogs, after all. "Let's go and find Jake, shall we?"

Cautiously Neil emerged into the courtyard, with Sam following him on a lead. He couldn't see his dad, but he could hear barking from the rescue centre, and he guessed Bob was in there. Swiftly he led the Border collie across the courtyard and out through the side gate. He didn't relax, or stop listening for his father's voice behind him, until he was down the drive and out onto the Compton road.

To begin with, Neil turned away from Compton, along the road for a little way, and then climbed over a stile leading to a footpath. That would take him in an almost direct line to the area he wanted to search. Sam hopped deftly over the stile behind him, reminding Neil of how clever he had once been at Agility competitions. He stood beside Neil on the other side, tongue lolling, head up as if he was asking, "Which way now?"

The footpath itself was obscured by snow, but the outline of it, alongside a hedge, was easy to follow, and from time to time there were small yellow waymarks, intended for country walkers. Neil knew this terrain well, but it was almost unrecognizable under its thick coat of snow. He felt thankful for the friendly dog trotting along beside him.

The smooth layer of fresh, untrodden snow covered uneven places in the ground, so Neil kept stumbling into holes he could not see. Snow trickled down over the tops of his boots and slowly began to turn his feet to lumps of ice. Once he slipped and fell. As he got up painfully, brushing snow off himself, he realized that he might get hurt. If he was stuck up here alone, probably no one would find him. He hadn't even left a note. For a few seconds he stood still, shivering and looking back. Had he done the right thing? Then, swallowing his fear, he went on.

His determination renewed, the going became easier as the footpath joined a farm track, where there were wheel marks for Neil and Sam to walk in. Before it reached the farm itself, another footpath led off to a second stile and a lane. Its surface was unmarked; no cars had been along there recently, but at least it was more solid underfoot.

Neil felt a rising excitement. He was getting close now to the area where he might expect to find his mum, Emily and Jake. He led Sam along the lane, uphill, because they would need to cross the ridge of moorland that surrounded Compton on this side.

They had not gone far when Neil realized that the sun had gone. Grey clouds were massing overhead again, and flakes of snow began to drift down, growing heavier with every step Neil took. He glanced down at Sam, padding undaunted alongside him.

"Thanks for sticking with me, boy. Not long now," he muttered.

As the bushes and trees on either side of the road thinned out, Neil became more conscious of the wind. It swirled snow in front of him so his eyes started to hurt as he tried to see his way. It drove snow into his face. His skin stung with it and his bare cheeks glowed bright red. He couldn't feel his feet any longer, and his hands were starting to go numb. He wound Sam's lead around his wrist, in case he should accidentally let go of the loop.

After what seemed like hours, but was

probably less than fifteen minutes, Neil realized that the upward slope was levelling out. They must be up on the ridge. He swallowed a gulp of snowfilled air, and bent down to pat Sam.

Snow was matted in Sam's coat, but the Border collie didn't seem at all bothered. He gave Neil's hand a friendly lick, and padded on into the wind. Neil began to wonder if he had been right to bring him.

He was finding it harder to see his way. The road stretched across the moor, with nothing on each side but a ditch. A few paces further on he tripped over a cattle grid, and barely saved himself from falling again. He kept veering from side to side, and only realized it when he saw the ditch open in front of him. Once he startled two or three sheep, huddling together in the shelter of a rock; they broke and ran off, bleating.

"Sorr-ee!" Neil cried after them.

Neil was so tired he could barely keep moving, but he knew it would be fatal to stop. People who were lost in the snow could lie down and go to sleep, and never get up again.

"We're not lost, are we, Sam?" he said, to comfort himself as much as the dog. "We know where we are."

He was beginning to feel really frightened, not for himself, but for Sam. How could he have been so stupid, to bring a sick dog out in weather like this? He should have known the snow would start again. He even stopped and peered round through the curtain of snow, but he could see nothing through the whirling whiteness. There was no shelter, and it was too late to go back.

As he went on, Neil realized that instead of walking correctly at heel, Sam had taken the lead. Instead of trying to guide them both through the snow, Neil started to follow. Straight away, the going was easier. He just had to keep on putting one foot in front of the other, shield his eyes as best he could from the driving snow, and let Sam find their way.

Soon they started to go downwards again. They crossed another cattle grid, and gradually more bushes appeared beside the road, sheltering Neil and Sam from the worst of the wind. It was easier for Neil to see, and he started to feel more hopeful; now he really might stand a chance of finding his family.

Not long after, they came to a crossroads. There was no sign to give Neil any idea of which direction to take, and Sam seemed to want to go straight on. Neil was too tired by now to do anything except let him have his way.

But about a hundred metres down the road, Neil had to stop. In front of him was a tumbled wall of snow, reaching above his head. Neil wasn't sure where it came from – blown there by the wind, or abandoned by a snow plough, or deposited like an avalanche from the hillside above. He only knew that there was no obvious way round it.

"Bad idea, Sam," he said.

Together he and the dog slogged back up the hill. Going over ground they had already covered made Neil feel even more exhausted.

When he reached the crossroads again, he stooped beside Sam. The Border collie stood with his head down. His breath was coming fast, and Neil could feel a rapid heartbeat. It was vital to find somewhere the dog could rest.

As he straightened up, Neil realized something else. Although the snow was slackening off, he could not see more than a few metres in any direction. Darkness was falling. The thought of how stupid he'd been hit Neil again. In the dark he wouldn't be able to find anything, not even his own way home.

"Left or right, Sam?" Neil asked. A lot depended on that decision. Sam just panted, obviously exhausted.

The left hand road looked as if it led up to the moor again. On the right the lane turned a sharp corner. Neil tugged on Sam's lead.

"OK, boy. Right it is."

This road twisted gradually downwards. Finally Neil came to a place where it seemed to zigzag back on itself and start leading back up.

"Oh, no," Neil groaned. Was he never going to get off the moor?

He kept trudging on, Sam padding wearily at his heels. Then as he came to the next bend, he halted. After rising a little way, the road dipped again.

And below him, at the bottom of the dip, barely visible in the dying light, was the King Street Kennels Range Rover.

"Mum!" Neil yelled. "Emily!"

Energy flooded through him again. Slipping and sliding, he dashed down the road. Seeming just as excited, Sam bounded after him. The slope was so steep that Neil was only able to stop when he crashed into the side of the car sending a wodge of snow sliding off the roof.

"Mum?" he said uncertainly.

The Range Rover was tipped forward, with its front wheels in a ditch at the side of the road. The windows were frosty on the outside and misted up inside. Neil dashed snow out of his eyes and scraped a circle of ice off one of the side windows. He tried to peer into the car, but he couldn't see anything.

"Mum!" he called, more loudly now.

He tried the driver's door, but it was locked. So was the rear door on the same side. Neil floundered through the snow around the back of the Range Rover. The ground gave way under him as he slid into the ditch. In his fall, he grabbed the handle of the rear door on the other side, and it swung open.

Apart from some crates of dog food, the Range Rover was completely empty. Carole and Emily and Jake were gone.

Chapter Eight

For a minute Neil stood and stared at the Range Rover. He couldn't think what to do. His plan didn't cover this.

He tried to work out where his mum, Emily and Jake might be. Perhaps they'd left the car and tried to walk home, and that was how Emily had been hurt. But his mum surely had more sense than to try doing that in heavy snow, especially when they had a small puppy to carry.

More likely, Neil thought, they'd been picked up, by the police or by a passing driver. Maybe they were safe at home now, while he was stuck here. Neil groaned aloud. His mum and dad would be furious with him when he got back!

But even that would be better than spending the night out here, and not getting home at all.

Neil used the car door to heave himself out of the ditch. Looking around in the gathering darkness he saw a spot of something bright on the snow further down the lane. "Stay, Sam," he said.

Leaving the Border collie to rest by the car, Neil struggled down the lane until he reached the bright object. When he picked it up, brushing snow off it, he saw it was Emily's crimson scarf. There were marks in the snow, too, though Neil could not make out what they were.

Just beside him was a five-barred gate; the snow was pushed away on the other side, as if someone had opened it recently. There were more marks on the hillside beyond, though the snow and the wind had partly erased them.

"Sam!" he called. "Sam!"

The Border collie came trotting towards him; Neil pointed up the hill. "Let's take a look, boy."

Sam squeezed through the space between the gate and the hedge, and scrambled away, scattering snow as he went. Neil clambered over the gate and struggled upwards in his wake, floundering in deep, loose drifts.

"Sam, wait for me!" he shouted.

Suddenly Sam was there again, pawing eagerly at his knees. Neil grabbed the lead. "You daft dog. What have you found?"

Sam let out a single bark, as if he was answering. Looking upwards, Neil could make out the shape of a building, black against the darkening sky. Hope surged through him, and died as he realized it wasn't a house, just a barn or a shed with blank walls.

"Sam, that's not—"

Neil's voice was cut off as Sam's bark sounded again, and as if in reply a light appeared ahead of them, by the dark building. Not light from a window; it looked more like a torch.

Neil took a few more paces, toiling up the hillside, feet slipping under him. Then he was flooded with relief as he started to make out the figure holding the torch, and heard a voice calling, "Neil? Is that you?"

It was Neil's mum.

The barn was stacked with bales of hay. Carole had pulled some of them out to make a cosy nest where Emily sat with one leg stretched out in front of her. Jake was curled up asleep in a blanket on her lap. But what made Neil stand gaping, when Carole guided him into shelter, was the other dog, lying nose on forepaws, by Emily's side. It was Denny.

"You've found him!" he exclaimed. "Is he OK?"

"Fine," said Emily. "He's lost his collar somehow, but he's not hurt."

"But what happened? What are you doing here?"

"I could ask you that," Carole said. "Coming out in weather like this by yourself was really stupid. And bringing Sam. What if you'd got lost?"

Neil wasn't going to tell her how close he had come, up on the moor. In fact, he felt so exhausted that he wasn't sure he could tell the story at all.

Carole must have seen how tired he was, because she stopped asking questions, just pushed him further into the barn and closed the door tightly against the harsh weather outside.

"OK," she said. "Our story first. But you'd better have a really good explanation when it's your turn."

She switched off the torch to save the battery and settled down in the hay beside Emily. Now the barn was dimly lit from windows high up under the roof. Neil collapsed on the floor on the other side of Denny. After so long out in the snow, the barn felt warm; he stripped off his gloves and pushed back the hood of his jacket.

To Neil's relief, Sam seemed none the worse for his struggle through the snow. He shook himself, scattering snow everywhere, and flopped down panting, his tongue hanging out in a satisfied grin. Neil grinned tiredly back.

"Go on, Mum," he said. "What happened?"

Carole began by telling Neil about the visit to Mike Turner, and how Mike had reassured them that Jake would be fine.

"Then we went to the Cash and Carry. That was fine, too. We bought what we needed and set off home. And that's where our problems started.

"There must have been some sort of accident or hold-up on the main road, because there was a queue of cars stretching right back to the bridge. We were about half an hour just inching along. So when we came to the turn-off on to the moor, I decided to be clever and drive home by the back roads."

She swiped a hand across her forehead, pushing away straggling dark hair.

"It was fine to start with. But the snow on the road was really thick, and even the Range Rover started to skid."

"And we ended up in the ditch," said Emily.

"So why didn't you stay with the car?" Neil asked. "I was scared stiff when I found it and you weren't there."

"You can thank Jake for that," Carole went on. "Emily and I got out to see if we could push the car out of the ditch. Not a hope, of course. We left Jake in the back, and then before we

90

knew what had happened, he'd taken off down the lane."

"I ran after him," Emily explained. "And I fell and sprained my ankle." She tried to move the outstretched leg, and winced.

"We'll hope it's just a sprain," Carole said. "Anyway, I chased after Jake, and I caught him just outside here. He was yapping fit to bust. And just before I started to carry him back to the car, I heard another dog barking inside. I had a look, and it was Denny!"

"Jake found him!" A beaming smile spread over Neil's face. "He's a real tracker dog!" He stared at the sleeping puppy. "I don't believe it!"

He guessed that Jake had just been feeling mischievous, but if his yapping had made Denny reply, that was good enough for Neil.

"So I helped Emily up here. I thought it would be warmer than the car," Carole went on. "That's when I tried to phone, but the battery was too low. I could kick myself for not bringing the spare with me."

Neil felt a sudden warm flood of triumph. He had almost forgotten about the mobile phone battery in all the confusion of the journey, but now he pulled it out of the pocket of his jeans.

"You mean this?" he asked innocently.

Carole stared at it. "Neil . . . you didn't? That's unbelievable! I thought we were stuck here all night, for sure."

She slid the mobile phone out of the inside pocket of her jacket, and fitted the spare battery. "Neil," she said as she punched in their home number, "I think you've just got yourself out of trouble."

Neil grinned. A few seconds later he heard a voice at the other end, as the phone was answered.

"Bob?" his mum said. "Yes, it's me. We're stuck in a barn somewhere. Neil found us and – oh." She flashed a look at Neil, and handed him the phone.

"Neil, I've been frantic!" Bob's voice came through clearly. "You shouldn't have gone off like that without asking."

"But you wouldn't have let me go," Neil protested. "And Mum and Emily would—"

"I've got the police out looking for you as well now!" his dad interrupted.

"Well . . ." Neil started to feel guilty. "I guess I could have left a note. But I'm fine, honestly, Dad. And you should have seen Sam! He—"

"Neil, put your mother on again. But don't think you've heard the last of this. We'll have a talk when you get home. A very serious one."

"OK, Dad. Bye."

Neil handed the phone back to his mum.

He was glad that he wasn't going home straight away. His dad probably needed some time to cool down – but Neil wasn't too worried about getting a stern dressing-down. He was confident he had done the right thing in setting out on his marathon journey with Sam.

Carole finished telling Bob what had happened, and then called the police to ask for help. Not really listening, Neil leant over to stroke the sleeping Jake.

"Beth and Gina will be over the moon," he said to Emily. "Do you think the pantomime will go on now?"

"Yes, I suppose . . ." Emily broke off, and her eyes filled with tears. "But I'll be out of it now, with this stupid ankle!"

"That's tough," said Neil. "I'm really sorry. Still," he added, "Denny's safe, and that's the main thing."

Emily sniffed, and nodded. "Yes, I know. But Neil, there's something else—"

She was interrupted again as Carole put the phone back into her pocket and said, "The

93

police are on their way. We'll be out of here before we know it."

"I hope so," Emily said. "That's what we haven't told you, Neil. When Mum found Denny in here the door was shut. There was no way he could have got in by himself."

"You mean someone shut him in here?" Neil asked.

Carole nodded. "I don't know why, but it looks as if somebody is keeping him here. And whoever he is, I really hope the police arrive before he gets back."

Chapter Nine

y now the barn was almost dark. Neil
could barely make out the shapes of
Emily and his mum or the dogs.
Everything was quiet except for little scuttling
noises in the hay, and an occasional snuffling
from Jake in his sleep.

"Neil," Carole said, "do you think you could
go down to the car and wait there for the police?
They shouldn't be long, and I don't want to miss
them."

"Er, sure," Neil said, groping to find the
gloves he had taken off.

Before he could get up they all heard
footsteps scrunch in the snow outside the barn,
and someone whistling a tune. Then both

footsteps and whistling stopped, and were followed by the sound of someone fumbling with the door catch. Emily audibly drew breath. Neil felt his heart start to pound. He got to his feet, and his mum switched on the torch as the door swung open.

A man stood in the entrance, shielding his eyes from the light. He was tall, wearing a long ragged overcoat tied round his waist with hairy string. Even though there was snow on the ground he wore scruffy trainers, which gaped at the toes. He carried a bulging plastic carrier bag.

Carole lowered the torch slightly and the man took his hand away from his eyes to reveal sharp features pinched with cold, surrounded by a bush of straggly white hair and beard. He was peering suspiciously at the Parkers.

"Who are you?" he asked. "What're you doing here?"

To Neil's surprise, it was Emily who replied. "Did you steal Denny?" she demanded fiercely. "The Wards aren't cruel to him. They're not!"

She tried to struggle upright and face him. Disturbed, Jake shot off her lap, yapping frantically, and hurled himself at the newcomer's trainers. Sam got to his feet, a low growling deep in his throat. Alarmed, the old man took a step back.

Only Denny stayed calm. He got up and trotted over to the man, who stooped and petted him, a smile spreading over his face.

"There's a good lad," he said. "Want to see what I've got for you?"

Neil started to realize that this wasn't an Animal Rights protester, even one crazy enough to steal a dog to make his point. And anyone who was that fond of a dog couldn't be all bad. Neil told Sam to sit, and scooped up Jake before he could make any more holes in the man's trainers.

"Emily, calm down." Carole had relaxed, as if she too realized that the newcomer was not a threat. "This dog belongs to some friends of ours," she told him. "They've been really worried."

"I didn't steal him, missus," the old man said. "I found him wandering. He weren't wearing a collar. I'd have taken him home if I'd known where he lived." He bent down again and scratched Denny's ears. "Denny's your name, eh? I called him Snowy," he explained, "cos it was snowing when I found him."

"He had a collar when he went missing." Emily was still suspicious. "And you could have taken him to the police."

"There weren't no hurry," the man said defensively. "Me and him, we found somewhere warm to stay, didn't we, lad? And then I went off to get us both something to eat."

He came further into the barn and started to rummage around in his carrier bag. From it he produced a rather soggy parcel and spread out the wrappings in front of Denny.

"There we are, lad. Nice bit o' liver."

Denny started to eat hungrily. Sam showed no interest, but Jake wriggled in Neil's arms, yipping in a frenzy, and the old man, his wrinkled face creased into a smile, gave him a scrap of the liver in his fingers.

"He's a fine little fellow," he said. "Is he yours, son?"

"Yes, his name's Jake. I'm Neil Parker, and this is my mum, Carole, and my sister Emily."

The old man ducked his head.

"Pleased to meet you, missus. They just call me Nick. I didn't mean no harm, you know," he said to Emily.

Emily smiled, but Neil thought she still didn't look entirely sure that she wanted to trust Nick. Neil suspected that the old man was lonely, and might have been putting off the time when he would have to give Denny up. At least he'd kept him safe, when he might have died of cold.

"You can come with us when we take him home," he said. "The Wards will want to thank you, and—"

He was interrupted by the sound of a car engine labouring through the snow on the road at the foot of the hill. Blue light flashed on and off in the darkness outside the barn door.

"The police," said Carole.

Nick looked terrified.

"It's OK," Neil said. "We didn't call them because of Denny. Just to shift our car out of the ditch."

"I'll go down." Carole handed the torch to Neil. "You stay here where it's warm, and keep the dogs out of the way."

When she had gone, Nick started to unload more bits and pieces from his carrier bag, as if he was going to settle in.

"You're not staying here, are you?" Neil asked. "Haven't you got anywhere to live?"

Nick shook his head. "I've been on the road for years. Reckon I wouldn't feel right no more with a roof over my head."

"But tomorrow's Christmas!" Emily protested.

Nick shrugged.

"You can't spend Christmas in a barn!"

Neil hid a quiet grin. The best way for Emily to stop being suspicious of Nick was for her to find out that he was in trouble. Emily couldn't resist helping – dogs, people, you name it.

"Why don't you come to stay with us for Christmas?" she continued. "Mum and Dad wouldn't mind, would they, Neil?"

Neil wasn't sure about that, but still . . . it was Christmas. "No, of course they wouldn't."

Nick frowned and shook his head. "Don't reckon I could do that. Wouldn't be right."

Another car engine roared into life. The Range Rover! Neil looked out of the door and saw the police van, its blue light whirling, and the Range Rover with its lights on. A policeman in a bright yellow jacket was moving between the two vehicles.

"They've fixed a tow rope," Neil reported to Emily, who was trying to persuade Nick to change his mind. "The Range Rover's not moving though. I wonder if—"

He broke off as the police van slowly moved backwards, and the Range Rover lurched and almost leapt backwards out of the ditch.

"Yes!" Neil said. "They've done it!"

He went on watching as very slowly and carefully his mum turned the Range Rover so that it faced towards the main road again. Then she got out and climbed the hill to the barn, closely followed by the policeman.

". . . so if you could help me get her into the car, I'll take her straight to our doctor," Neil heard her say as she came into earshot.

"No problem," the policeman said, clapping

his hands together. He was a huge young man with a friendly grin. "Good heavens, you've got a right collection here, haven't you?" The grin faded as his eyes fell on Nick. "Who's this, then? He's not with you, is he?"

"Yes, he is!" Emily said, flying to Nick's defence.

"I'm not doing no harm," Nick said. "Just sheltering from the snow."

"Well, you can't shelter here, mate," the policeman said. "This is private property. You'll have to move on."

"In this?" Carole said. "Oh, come on, officer. You're not going to throw somebody out into the snow on Christmas Eve?"

The young policeman looked uncomfortable. "I'm sorry, ma'am, but the law's the law. There's a fire hazard, for one thing, if he stays here. Come on, mate. Let's go."

Muttering under his breath, Nick had already started to pack up his belongings into the plastic bag.

"Mum," Neil said, "this is horrible. Can't he come and stay with us for Christmas?"

"Please, Mum!" Emily added.

"Well . . ."

Carole was starting to smile, but the

policeman interrupted her. "It's not a good idea, ma'am, if I may say so."

"No you may not," Carole said crisply. "Who I invite into my house is my affair. This gentleman has already been very helpful in looking after our friends' dog, and if he wants to come to stay with us he's very welcome. Please come and spend Christmas with us, Nick."

Nick still looked doubtful, glancing from Carole to the policeman and back again. Inspired, Neil said, "We run King Street Kennels. We've got lots of dogs for you to meet."

"You could give us a hand with them if you like," said Carole.

Nick's face lit up, and creased again into a pleased smile. "Well, missus, if you're sure . . ."

"That's settled then," said Carole. "Now, officer, if you could just give Emily a hand, we can all get moving."

Everyone slowly made their way down the hill towards the waiting cars. Carole went first, followed by the policeman carrying Emily. Nick came next with Sam and Denny padding after him. Last of all, closing the barn door carefully behind him, came Neil with Jake bundled inside his jacket. He wasn't going to risk the little dog running off again.

The policeman helped Emily into the back of the Range Rover, and went back to his own van where another policeman was waiting.

"I was going to take you to Casualty," Carole explained to Emily. "But the policeman tells me they've got queues a mile long. So I rang Dr Harvey, and he says that if we go round there he'll see us at home. He's already closed for the holidays." Briskly she added, "Neil, can you get the dogs into the back? Nick, you sit next to me."

When he was in the back of the car, surrounded by dogs, Neil leant over and murmured into Emily's ear, "Don't you there's something funny about this? Nick – Nicholas – bushy white beard . . .?"

Emily started to giggle, but the engine starting up covered the sound.

"Better hope Squirt doesn't catch on," Neil added. "She always said Father Christmas would bring Denny back!"

Chapter Ten

D r Harvey gently examined Emily's ankle.

"You've got a nasty sprain there," he said. "But that's all it is. I'm sure it's not broken. I'll put a bandage on it, and you've got to stay off the foot as much as you can for the next few days."

"Thank goodness it's no worse," said Carole.

The Parkers were huddled round the fire in Alex Harvey's sitting room. Finn and Sandy, the doctor's two dogs, lay on the hearthrug and watched his every move. Finn was a Kerry blue, a real show dog, while Sandy was just an ordinary mutt, but now that the two of them had settled down together they were the best of friends, and Alex loved them both.

Carole had left Sam and Denny in the car with Nick to look after them, but Neil had insisted on bringing Jake inside. The tiny Border collie scrambled around on his lap, eager to get down and make friends, but Neil kept him firmly out of the way. Finn at least could be a bit uncertain in temper at times. Besides, Neil didn't dare think what Jake might do with a bandage!

"You've got a lively one there," Dr Harvey said as he fastened Emily's bandage in place. He leant over and tickled Jake. "Are we going to see him winning all the Agility prizes like his dad?"

"Maybe," Neil said.

"No, he's a tracker dog," Emily contradicted.

Dr Harvey laughed. "Is he really? Isn't he a bit small for a bloodhound?"

"You could try training him for obedience *and* tracking events," Carole said. "But there's time enough to think about that when he's bigger. Let's get Christmas over first." She got up and started to put her coat back on. "Are you going away for Christmas, Alex?"

Dr Harvey looked gloomy.

"I was going over to my sister and her family in York. But all the roads across the Pennines are closed because of the snow. I'll never get there now."

"That's awful!" said Emily. She exchanged a look with her mother and Neil. "Mum, couldn't we . . ."

"Yes, of course we could. Alex, you're coming to have Christmas dinner with us. And Finn and Sandy, of course."

The doctor's face broke into a smile. "If you're sure . . ."

"No problem. Bob bought a turkey big enough to feed half of Compton. You're very welcome, Alex."

"Then in that case . . ." Alex Harvey's grin broadened, "we'd be delighted. All three of us."

"Ace!" said Neil.

"Come about twelve noon," Carole said as the doctor carried Emily out to the car. "Things should be livening up about then."

Neil looked up at the sky. The snow had almost stopped, though a few stray flakes were still drifting down.

"I hope you don't get stuck," he said.

"Don't worry," Dr Harvey promised. "I'll get there. Even if I have to borrow a sledge and harness Finn and Sandy!"

*

107

Back in the car, Carole turned for home.

"We'll drop Denny off on the way," she said. "It's a good thing it's not far."

The lights were on in the Wards' house when the Range Rover pulled up outside. Neil hurried up the path and rang the bell. Emily refused to stay in the car and hobbled after Nick and Carole who had brought Denny.

Beth Ward opened the door and stood frozen, staring at Denny at Nick's feet.

"Oh it is!" she said at last. "Oh, thank you! You've really found him."

"Beth?" It was Gina's voice. "Who are you—"

She came up the passage behind Beth, and broke off as she saw Denny. The retriever bounded away from Nick, barking eagerly and licking Gina's face as she hugged him.

"Easy to see he's yours," Nick said, a bit sadly.

"But where did you find him?" Beth asked. "His collar's gone – and Emily, what happened to you? Oh, come in, everybody, and tell us all about it."

They all crowded into the Wards' tiny kitchen. Gina went to fetch her mother to hear the good news, while Beth found a chair for Emily. Neil let Jake and Sam roam around while he and Emily told the story, with additions now and again from their mother and Nick.

"So it's you we've really got to thank," Mrs Ward said to Nick, when they had finished. "I'm sure Denny would have died of cold if you hadn't looked after him. You naughty boy!" she added to Denny. "Don't you dare wander off like that again!"

Denny, with his face in a bowl of food, didn't

seem too bothered by the scolding. Mrs Ward took out her purse and emptied it of notes, which she held out to Nick.

"Don't be offended," she said. "But I'm sure you can make good use of this. And Denny's worth ten times as much to us."

Nick grinned. "I don't offend easy, missus." He took the notes and stowed them away inside his ragged overcoat. "Thanks. It were a pleasure to look after him. He's a grand dog."

"He's really clever!" Emily said. "Beth, show Nick some of Denny's tricks."

Denny had finished feeding, so Beth snapped her fingers to get his attention, shook hands with him, and made him beg for a biscuit and jump over her outstretched arm.

"It's silly to think he doesn't enjoy it," Emily said.

"I wouldn't force him," Beth said, petting Denny and rewarding him with a biscuit. "All right, trouble, here you are," she added to Jake, who trotted up to her and pushed his nose into her hand. She gave him a biscuit, and one to Sam, who had better manners, but was looking on hopefully. "At least now we can forget about that horrid phone call. It wasn't anything to do with Animal Rights at all."

"Glen told us none of his friends would steal a dog," said Emily.

"So all we have to worry about now is the pantomime," said Gina.

"Will it still go on?" Neil asked.

"Yes, of course it will!" Beth sounded cheerful and determined. "We've still got a week. Now that Denny's back we can do anything! Emily, I'll give you a ring about rehearsals on Boxing Day, OK?"

"But I've hurt my ankle," Emily said. Neil could see she was trying hard not to cry. "I can't be in it."

"Oh, yes, you can," said Beth. "I'm not having you drop out now; not when you've done so much to get Denny back."

"Dr Harvey says I mustn't walk on it."

"Then you can do your part sitting down." Beth refused to be put off. "Don't worry, I'll work it out. You can still sing, can't you?"

Emily started to smile, even though she had to wipe away a tear or two. Neil and the others pretended not to notice.

"And another thing, Neil," Beth went on. "I've been thinking. When we do the pantomime there are a lot of scenes where Denny isn't on. I've too much to do to look after him myself, and so has Gina, so I need somebody to be responsible for him. How would you like to be the pantomime's official dog handler?"

Neil stared at her. He'd resigned himself to being out of the pantomime altogether. Now he felt so pleased he thought he was going to burst.

"Dog handler?" he echoed. "You bet! That's what I do best!"

On the way home the roads were dark and silent. Very few cars were out. Carole drove slowly and carefully; the snow gleamed an eerie white in the car headlights. At long last the Range Rover turned into the drive of King Street Kennels.

"Made it!" said Carole.

As she switched off the engine the front door opened and Bob came down the steps.

"Are you all right?" he asked. "What took so long?"

Carole passed a hand over her face. Neil thought that she looked tired.

"It's a long story," she said. "I'll tell you in a few minutes. Can you take Emily indoors, while we put this dog food away?"

"Sure." Bob swung Emily up into his arms

and carried her off up the steps into the house. Neil thought he hadn't even noticed Nick.

Everyone else got out of the car. Neil had to give Sam a shove from behind; the Border collie had fallen asleep during the drive, but Neil thought he was none the worse for his excursion. He followed Neil through the side gate, while Carole and Nick unloaded the cases of dog food Carole had bought at the Cash and Carry.

Neil went to open up the store for his mother and Nick to begin stacking boxes, but the room already looked full.

"The Preston's van must have been," Carole said, pushing a strand of hair out of her eyes. "Wouldn't you just know! I needn't have gone to the Cash and Carry at all."

"And then we wouldn't have found Denny," Neil pointed out. "Or Nick."

From his cosy nest in Neil's jacket, Jake gave a little yap of agreement.

"All right, mutt," Neil said affectionately. "We all know you found him really."

It didn't take long for the extra food to be stored and Carole to close up the store room. Nick said to her:

113

"I see you've got a barn, missus."

"That's right."

"Mebbe I could sleep there, instead of in the house? I don't feel right under a roof. I've not slept in a proper bed for years."

"Well . . ."

Carole was hesitating, but Neil thought Nick's idea was a really good one. The barn was partially heated, and there was plenty of straw there, kept for the dogs' bedding. Nick could have blankets and a sleeping bag from the house. Now that he thought about it, Neil wouldn't have minded spending the night there himself.

"Emily'd be pleased," he said. "She won't have to share with Squirt."

"Well, Nick, if it's really what you'd prefer . . ." Carole said.

Nick's creased smile reappeared. "That'd be just grand, missus."

As they crossed the courtyard to the back door, Bob appeared. He bent down, stroked Sam's head, and felt for his heartbeat.

"Seems OK," he said, "but it wasn't a good idea to take him out like that, Neil. We'll keep an eye on him for a day or two, and if there seems to be a problem we'll call Mike."

He let Sam go, and the Border collie slipped past him into the house. Bob shook hands with Nick.

"Hello. Emily told me you looked after Denny. Welcome to King Street. I hear you're spending Christmas with us?"

"Seems like it, mister." Nick touched his forehead as if he might have lifted his cap to Bob. "And your missus says I might help with the dogs, like. I love dogs."

"That's fine, Nick. I'm sure we can find you some odd jobs to do."

While Nick and Bob were talking, Carole was tapping her foot impatiently. "Bob," she said, "do you think we could all go inside and get warm?"

"Yes – yes, of course." For the first time Neil thought his father was looking a bit agitated. Surely nothing else could go wrong now? "You see the Preston's delivery came?" his dad asked, still standing in the doorway. "Not long ago. I'd just about given them up."

"Yes, Bob," Carole said, starting to sound irritated. "But do we have to talk about it out here?"

"And there was an e-mail." Now Neil was sure his dad was talking for the sake of talking.

What was there inside the house that he didn't want Carole to see? "An e-mail from John Cartwright," Bob went on wildly. "He wishes us a Happy Christmas, and he says he's enjoying the sun, but it really isn't the same without Bernie. Next year he says he's going to be spending Christmas with his best friend."

Neil had to think about that, even while he wondered about his dad's strange behaviour. He'd imagined how pleased John Cartwright would be if he had managed to make Bernie into a proper rescue dog. But he'd failed so far. And now he realized that Bernie was already far more special than just another rescue dog. He was John Cartwright's best friend. Bernie didn't *need* any extra training.

"Bob," said Carole, with exaggerated patience, "why are we standing on the back step in the freezing cold talking about John Cartwright's e-mail?"

Bob looked sheepish. "There's something I should tell you—"

He grabbed at Carole's arm as she headed past him, missed, and made a face at Neil as they all trooped into the kitchen with Carole in the lead. Neil almost cannoned into his mum as she halted in the doorway.

"Bob!" she said. "What have you done?"

Peering round his mum, Neil stared into the kitchen. It was warm and bright. Delicious cooking smells were wafting from huge pots on top of the stove. At the kitchen table Emily was seated, with her injured foot on a stool. Sarah was sitting on the floor beside Sam's basket. Both had beaming smiles on their faces. But none of that was what made Neil stare.

The kitchen was full of dogs. Sam was in his basket. Two tiny white puppies, younger even than Jake, were scrambling all over Sarah and licking her face. A bull terrier with a white clown's face peered round the side of the old basket chair by the window. An Afghan hound, elegant and long-haired, was sprawled over most of the free floor space, while a black Scottie sat beside Emily, stumpy tail wagging as she scratched his wiry coat.

Carole blinked. "Bob – tell me I'm dreaming."

"Sorry," said Bob.

"These are the rescue dogs. What are they all doing in here?"

"That's what I was trying to tell you. The heating has gone off in the rescue centre, and I don't know what the matter is. And I won't be able to get an engineer out until after Christmas." He spread his arms. "I had to put them somewhere."

But Bob . . ." Carole still looked appalled. "Bob, I've invited Alex Harvey for Christmas lunch. He'll bring Finn and Sandy as well."

"More dogs!" Sarah was delighted. "Lots of dogs for Christmas!"

Suddenly Carole's laughter bubbled up. She stood there shaking with it.

"If this is a dog's life," she gasped out when she could speak again, "then I can't get enough of it!"

Bob gave her a hug and went to start serving out the supper. Neil picked his way around assorted dogs to put Jake down beside Sam and fetch some food and water. He was turning back with the full bowls when he saw that Jake had grabbed Bob's slipper and was shaking it fiercely, growling and gnawing with tiny teeth.

"That's right, Jake," Neil said. "Save us from Dad's killer stinky slipper!"

He grinned across the kitchen at Emily, who grinned back.

"This is going to be a great Christmas," she said.

"A great Christmas," Neil agreed. "A real, doggy, Puppy Patrol Christmas!"

Look out for Puppy Patrol No. 16:

Puppy Love

It's love at first sight!

When Sarah Parker rescues a lost puppy from a badger set, it's love at first sight! Digger is the nicest puppy in the world – and she wants him to stay at King Street Kennels for ever.

But there's danger on the loose in Compton. And soon Digger may need rescuing again – from trouble that's very close to home . . .

Puppy Patrol titles available from
Macmillan Children's Books

The prices shown below are correct at the time of
going to press. However, Macmillan Publishers
reserve the right to show new retail prices on covers
which may differ from those previously advertised.